ITASCA COMMUNITY LIBRARY

500 W. IRVING PARK ROAD

ITASCA, IL 60143

1/15 8

Safari Animals™

GIRAFFES

Amelie von Zumbusch

PowerKiDS press™

New York

Published in 2007 by The Rosen Publishing Group, Inc.
29 East 21st Street, New York, NY 10010

First Edition

Book Design: Erica Clendening
Layout Design: Julio Gil

Photo Credits: Cover, pp. 1, 5, 17, 23 © Artville; pp. 7, 13, 15, 19, 21, 24 (top left, top right, bottom right) © Digital Vision; pp. 9, 11, 24 (bottom left) © Digital Stock.

Library of Congress Cataloging-in-Publication Data

Zumbusch, Amelie von.
  Giraffes / Amelie von Zumbusch. — 1st ed.
     p. cm. — (Safari animals)
  Includes index.
  ISBN-13: 978-1-4042-3615-8 (library binding)
  ISBN-10: 1-4042-3615-5 (library binding)
  1. Giraffe—Juvenile literature. I. Title.
  QL737.U56Z86 2007
  599.638—dc22
                                        2006019454

Manufactured in the United States of America

CONTENTS

The tallest animal on Earth is the giraffe. Giraffes can be up to 18 feet (5.5 m) tall.

5

Giraffes live on the grasslands of Africa.

Giraffes have very long necks. They also have long legs.

9

Giraffes have patterns on their coats. Each giraffe has a different pattern.

Each giraffe has two small horns on its head. A giraffe's horns are covered with hair.

13

Giraffes eat leaves. Their long necks let them reach the high leaves on tall trees.

The leaves of the acacia tree are the food giraffes like best.

Giraffes get water from the leaves they eat. They also drink water from water holes.

Giraffes move across the grasslands in small groups.

A baby giraffe is called a calf. A giraffe calf is already 6 feet (2 m) tall when it is born.

23

Words to Know

grasslands

horns

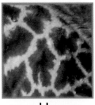

pattern

water hole

Web Sites

Due to the changing nature of Internet
links, PowerKids Press has developed an
online list of Web sites related to this
book. This site is updated regularly. Plea
use this link to access the list:
www.powerkidslinks.com/safari/giraffe,